For Scriveners Ink
H.B.

For Jana
J.O.

VIKING
Published by the Penguin Group
Penguin Books Ltd, 27 Wrights Lane, London W8 5TZ, England
Penguin Books USA Inc., 375 Hudson Street, New York, New York 10014, USA
Penguin Books Australia Ltd, Ringwood, Victoria, Australia
Penguin Books Canada Ltd, 10 Alcorn Avenue, Toronto, Ontario, Canada M4V 3B2
Penguin Books (NZ) Ltd, 182–190 Wairau Road, Auckland 10, New Zealand

Penguin Books Ltd, Registered Offices: Harmondsworth, Middlesex, England

First published in the USA by Lothrop, Lee & Shepard Books 1994
Published in Great Britain by Viking 1995
1 3 5 7 9 10 8 6 4 2

Filmset in Goudy

PRINTED IN BELGIUM BY

INTERNATIONAL BOOK PRODUCTION

A CIP catalogue record for this book is available from the British Library

ISBN 0-670-86374-2

GRANDMOTHER
AND I

HELEN E. BUCKLEY • JAN ORMEROD

VIKING

Grandmother and I
are sitting in the big chair, rocking.
We rock back and forth, and back and forth.
And Grandmother hums little tunes.
And her shoes make a soft sound on the floor.

Other people have laps too.
Mothers' laps are good
when there's not enough room on the bus.
Or when you need to have your shoes tied.
And your hair braided.

Fathers' laps are good
when you want to be a cowboy.
Or do tricks.

But Grandmother's lap is just right
when you're having a bad cold.
We sit in the big chair
and rock back and forth, and back and forth.
And Grandmother hums little tunes.
And her shoes make a soft sound on the floor.

Brothers and sisters
let you ride
on their backs...

but when they read out loud to you,
*they want you to sit **beside** them.*

But Grandmother's lap is just right
when lightning is coming in the window.
We sit in the big chair
and rock back and forth, and back and forth.
And Grandmother hums little tunes.
And her shoes make a soft sound on the floor.

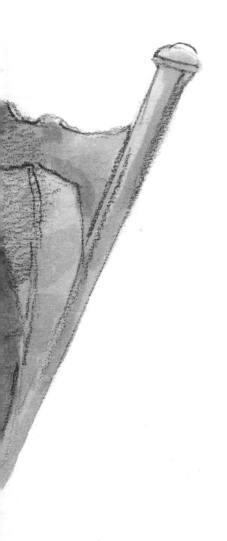

Grandfathers' laps are good
after you've been for a walk.
Or when you want to count the cars
going by.

But Grandmother's lap is just right
when the cat's been gone for two days,
and you don't want to do anything
but sit in the big chair,
and rock back and forth, and back and forth,
while Grandmother hums little tunes.
And her shoes make a soft sound on the floor...

make
soft
sounds
on
the
floor.